Bedtime Hullabaloo!

Bedtime Hullabaloo!

Written by David Conway
Illustrated by Charles Fuge
First published in hardback in 2010 by
Hodder Children's Books
This paperback edition published in 2011

Text copyright © David Conway 2010
Illustrations copyright © Charles Fuge 2010
Hodder Children's Books
338 Euston Road
London, NW1 3 BH

Hodder Children's Books Australia
Level 17/207 Kent Street
Sydney, NSW 2000

ISBN: 978 1 444 93927 9

Printed in China

Hodder Children's Books is a division
of Hachette Children's Books.
An Hachette UK Company.

www.hachette.co.uk

CHARLES FUGE AND DAVID CONWAY

Bedtime Hullabaloo!

Hodder Children's Books

A division of Hachette Children's Books

ONE NIGHT IN THE SILLY SAVANNAH

a ludicrous leopard was leapfrogging to bed when all of a sudden there was a terrible racket...

'What a hullabaloo!' said the leopard
and decided to follow the noise.

Along the way the leopard passed by a dozy giraffe singing a lullaby when all of a sudden...

HHHRRR-ZZZ!

SNORT, SNORT!

'What a hullabaloo!' said the giraffe and decided to follow the noise.

The leopard and
the giraffe then met a
baboon who was reading
a bedtime story to the moon
when all of a sudden...

HHHRRR-ZZZ!

SNORT, SNORT!

GRUNT, GRUNT!

'What a hullabaloo!'
said the baboon and decided
to follow the noise.

The three animals followed the noise
to check out all the fuss and discover
the source of this bedtime din, this
clamour, this hubbub, this rumpus.

Under the still starlit night they walked.
The noise began to swell.

More and more animals joined in the search
to seek out the nuisance as well. There was
a hat-wearing hyena half asleep, a music-making
meerkat counting sheep...

...a zany zebra who was having a dream about sailing upon a sea of ice cream,

a sleepwalking lion with bedraggled hair,
an outraged ostrich clutching a teddy bear,
and a polka-dot, pyjama-wearing water buffalo.

So on they all walked into the night, all sleepy and tired and very uptight. Through the long giggling grass, past the tickling tree.

and when at last they came to a stop what on earth did they see?

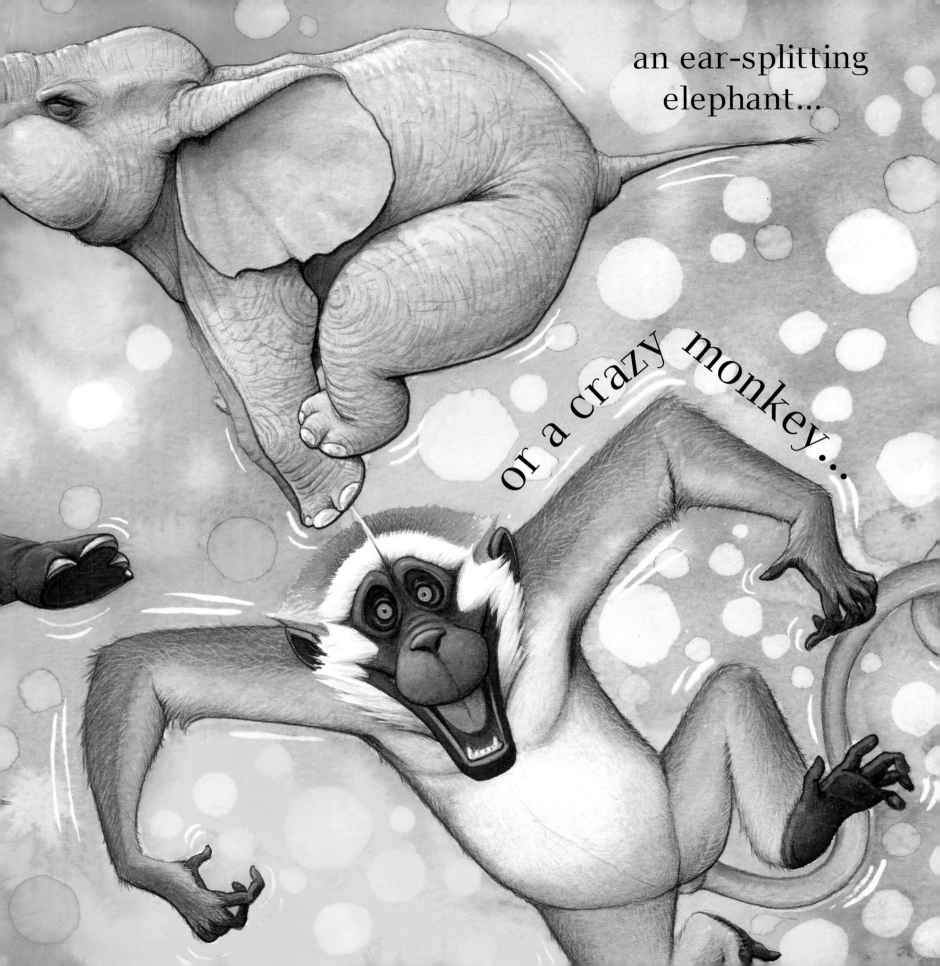

But a tiny shrew, wearing a pink tutu, snoring her head off very loudly.

HHHRRR-ZZZ!

SNORT, SNORT! GRUNT, GRUNT!

Something had to be done. Leopard growled as loud as he could. Giraffe bleated even louder.

Baboon screeched with
all his might until...

...the terrible racket woke the shrew from her thunderous slumber.

And all was quiet on the Silly Savannah,
so quiet you couldn't hear a peep...

...until the silence was suddenly shattered
by some animals fast asleep in a heap.

R-ZZZ!

SNORT,
SNORT!

GRUNT,
GRUNT!

SNUFFLE,
SNUFFLE!

BUT NOT FOR LONG!